NO GROOM
AT THE INN

USA Today Bestselling Author
KATHLEEN LAWLESS

Cover design by Sweet'n'Spicy Designs
ISBN 978-1-989873-21-2
Print ISBN 978-1-989873-72-4

Table of Contents

DEDICATION

Fellow romance author and shopping maven,
Marcia King Gamble

Chapter 1

Meredith's attention drifted from the meeting room to the window and beyond, where sunlight blazed in a blue sky and a tropical breeze sent the palm trees swaying. It was hard to believe it was less than one week until Christmas. She half-listened as the other managers at the Four Seasons – Hualalai droned on about their departments' roles for the upcoming week. Christmas holidays were always a busy time at the resort, an excuse she used every year to not go home and be with her family in soggy Seattle.

"Right, Meredith?" said the front desk manager, pulling her out of her thoughts and back to the present.

"For sure," she said, wondering what she had just agreed to. Chloe, her assistant scribbled *stockings* and tilted the note her way. "Chloe's got that handled," she added. "I've been focused on Bridezilla."

Across the room, Asher, the Activities Director smirked. He would.

"There's always one of those," the catering manager said sympathetically.

Chloe interrupted. "For the stockings, if I could have the complete guest list, ages of the children and room numbers the day before, that would be awesome."

Awesome! Had Meredith ever been that young? Sure didn't feel like it.

Around the room, the other managers stirred and began closing their laptops or notebooks, signaling the meeting's end. Meredith rose just as the GM's secretary poked her head in the door. "Mer, when you're done, there's someone here to see you."

Probably Bridezilla. "Tell whoever it is I'll be right out."

Asher paused next to her. "Try not to take everything so seriously."

Meredith did an exaggerated batting of her eyes at the man who was every woman's wet dream.

Including hers, not that she'd ever admit it to him. "Be more like you, you mean? I'm the wrong gender to be pouring on the charm to the female guests the way you do."

Asher gave her his trademark, drop-dead gorgeous smile that sent women of all ages into a swoon. "Can I help it if the fairer sex finds me irresistible?"

Just the way he said 'sex' sent a tingle to her girl parts. In the three years since they both started working here, she'd perfected her technique to treat Asher like the brother she never had. Much safer that way. "No, but I'd prefer if you didn't flaunt it quite so blatantly."

"Hey, I've talked more than one of your brides down off the chandelier."

Meredith arched her brow in acknowledgement. She'd love to hate the guy, but every word was the truth. He'd started work here the same time she had, and they'd become buddies over the years, which was the only safe way to be around Asher.

"Why don't you come with me?" Meredith said. "Maybe all Bridezilla needs is a reassuring pat on the head and your famous smile."

"You know you can count on me," he said, resting one arm on her hip in that familiar, friendly way he had with everyone, resort staff and guests of all ages.

True. But it was better if she didn't start to count on him too much.

When they reached the hotel's main reception area, Meredith froze.

"What is it?" Asher asked, just as a chorus of voices yelled, "Surprise!"

"*Omg!*" Meredith turned to Asher in dismay. "My family!"

They were all there, rushing toward her, her chubby, blonde mother leading the charge ahead of her two sisters. Her father and brothers-in-law followed at a more sedate pace while Theresa's two kids trailed behind, trying to look cool.

"What are you doing here?" she said as they converged on her and Asher, everyone talking at once.

"Since you never make it home for Christmas, we decided to come to you." Her mother reached her first and hugged her, her smile widening as she transferred her attention to Asher. "And *this* must be Asher!" She abandoned Meredith to throw her arms around Meredith's companion. Over her mother's head Asher gave her a puzzled look as he returned the hug.

"Nice to meet you, Mrs. Robb."

"Oh, silly boy. So formal. I insist you call me, Helen." She pinched his cheek as if he was a youngster. "You're even more handsome than in your pictures."

Meredith pressed her lips tightly together and tried to ignore the amused glint in Asher's turquoise blue eyes.

"You didn't tell me you sent your mom pictures."

Meredith mumbled something unintelligible as her father stepped forward and claimed his hug, followed by her sisters.

5

"This is certainly a surprise," she said, after she finally extricated herself. "I should do the introductions. Asher, you've met my mom. This is my dad, Bill. Theresa," she pointed, "and her husband Dave and their two kids. Emily over there next to her husband, Michael." She forced a smile. "How long will you all be here?"

"Almost a week," Helen said brightly.

"I wish I'd known," Meredith said. "It's such a busy time right now, a ton of weddings and other events that I'm just swamped. But I'm sure you'll all have a nice time."

Helen linked her arm through Meredith's. "That's part of the surprise. I called your boss and explained things to him and he's agreed to give you a week off. He said your assistant is more than capable of handling the department."

Explained things? What things?

"A week off?" Meredith echoed, dumbfounded. Chloe would love that. She'd been after Meredith's job even before it was Meredith's. "I'm not sure that's such a good idea."

6

"Of course it is. No one can be expected to work all the time."

"I've been telling her the same thing," Asher said in his not-exactly-helpful way. "All work and no play."

"Exactly!" Helen beamed. "And when I explained the situation, your nice boss, Mr. Yoshi, granted Asher some time off as well."

"Situation?" Asher asked.

Helen poked Asher's upper arm. "I have to hand it to you two. Such discretion. No one I spoke to had any idea you two were dating, let alone getting engaged."

"Mom, I—"

"Oops," Helen pressed her fingers to her lips. "I know it's not official yet, but you did imply—"

"What did Meredith tell you?" Asher asked with mock innocence.

Oh, how she longed to wipe that smug look off his face!

"Just that you two have been dating for nearly three years and things are looking serious.

Something to that effect."

Asher moved closer and tucked his arm around Meredith's waist, as he smiled down at her. "I didn't know you'd told your mom about us, sweetheart. I thought we agreed to keep it a secret."

"Oh, don't blame Meredith. I pried it out of her," Helen said. "We've all been so worried, ever since—"

"We should see if your rooms are ready," Meredith said. "I bet you're dying to get settled and hit the beach."

* * *

By the time her family had their luggage sorted, keys in hand, and were headed for the elevators, Meredith felt like she'd been run over by a hurricane. And she couldn't ditch Asher, who dogged her heels all the way to her office.

"What kinds of things does your family like to do?" he asked.

Meredith furrowed her brow. "What do you mean?"

"Surfing? Fishing? Kayaking? I'll line up

some fun things for them while they're here."

Meredith turned to him, hugging her laptop to her chest as if it was body armor. "Listen, Ash, you don't have to do this. I'll explain it was all a misunderstanding and—"

He cocked a brow. "You've been telling them for three years I'm your boyfriend and things are getting serious. That's pretty hard to brush off as a misunderstanding."

Meredith flopped into the chair behind her desk. "I never dreamed they'd just show up unannounced."

"You've got no worries, Mer. I've got your back."

"No, really—"

"We're friends, right?"

Meredith nodded.

"And friends help each other out in a jam, right?"

"I guess."

"I don't mind having a week off to play tour guide."

She gave him a long look. "It's more than tour guide."

"Oh!" That smirk was back. "You mean the challenge of pretending to be your lover?"

"Quit enjoying this quite so much."

"I've been telling you for years that you take life too seriously. That you need to let your hair down and have a little fun once in a while."

Meredith straightened. "Some of us don't think of life as one big playground."

He reached over and clucked her under the chin. "It's only for a week. Think you can pretend to like me? Even a little?"

Meredith sighed. No *pretense involved. The hard part would be keeping her feelings hidden.*

"I don't want any of your real girlfriends to get mad," she drawled. "I'm sure you have holiday plans with several of them."

"Let me worry about that," he said smoothly. "In the meantime, I invited the family to my place for dinner tonight."

"You did *what?*"

He shrugged unapologetically. "I'm not supposed to make a good impression on my future in-laws?"

For once in her life, Meredith was speechless.

* * *

Asher was down in the boatshed checking the rigging on one of the resort's baby catamarans used by the guests when Joel, his second-in-command, found him.

"There you are," Joel said. "Is everything okay?"

"Sure. Why?" Asher asked.

"Yoshi said you're taking some vacation time. Family stuff. I wondered if maybe you have to fly home."

"Nothing like that," Asher said. "Meredith's family surprised her with a visit and I'm giving her a hand showing them around."

Joel gave him a long, telling look. "For real?"

"Pretty much. I figure you can hold down the fort." Joel had been standoffish when Asher first started working here and it had taken a while to break through his resentment when Asher beat him out for the head job, but out of that rocky start sprang a solid friendship. Plus, they were from the same home town high school.

"Why do I smell something you're not telling me?" Joel said.

"Because you're suspicious by nature?"

"If my folks showed up here for a vacation, I'm pretty sure I could deal with them myself without dragging you into the mix."

Asher shrugged. "I guess Meredith has a different relationship with her family than you do with yours."

"Ah, meaning a healthy dose of the Ash-Man charm is in order. Is she trying to set you up with some mutt of a sister?"

"For the record, each of Mer's sisters has a husband in tow."

Joel's gaze narrowed. "I know!" he said. "You're the beard."

"What?" Asher said.

"You're Meredith's fake date to get her family

off her back about how come she's still single while everyone else is paired up."

"Something like that, maybe," Asher said, uncomfortable with the turn of the conversation.

"So if I see you two holding hands and acting all lovey-dovey, I'm supposed to pretend that's normal."

"Don't you have some kayaks or paddleboards to haul in off the beach?" Asher asked.

"Maybe it won't be much of an act for you," Joel said.

Asher lobbed a ball of marine rope his way. "Meredith and I are friends. Friends help friends out."

"Maybe the lady would have given you a look before this if you didn't pretend so hard to be setting the world record for the highest number of dates in a single year."

"Joel!" Asher said warningly.

Joel raised his hands playfully in the air. "I'm going. I just don't want you to get hurt along the way."

"Me? Teflon Man?"

"Don't forget, Teflon Man," Joel said. "I knew you when."

Ash nodded at Joel's retreating back. Joel had been a couple of years behind him in school and their paths hadn't crossed at the time, but Joel was the one person here who knew about Asher's secret past.

Chapter 2

Meredith poured herself a glass of wine and settled in for what she expected to be a very long evening—the first of *how many?*— with her family.

"You have a lovely home, Asher," Helen said looking around at Asher's pleasant, three-bedroom bungalow with its wrap-around, covered lanai.

"Have you lived here long?"

Meredith's mouth watered as Asher opened the lid on the grill, filling the air with the smell the fresh pineapple and Mai-Mai cooking.

"Thank you, Helen," Asher said. "I bought it sight unseen just before I moved here."

Helen shot Meredith a look. "Meredith stayed in that dreadful staff accommodation at the resort before she bought her condo, but I always maintained she would have been better off if she had bought a house. Do you two have any plans to live together?" she continued as she sipped a frosty glass of Asher's signature rum punch.

"I never wanted the maintenance that goes with owning a home," Meredith said tightly. "I moved here to surf when I'm not working, not do upkeep on a house and yard."

"Do *you* surf?" Helen asked Asher.

"I sure do. Hon," he said to Meredith, "would you mind tossing the salad and bringing out the plates and cutlery. My table's not big enough for all of us to sit there so I hope everyone's all right with eating on their lap."

Meredith escaped into the kitchen where she spent several fruitless minutes trying to find things. For a guy, Asher had a lot of kitchen gadgets and utensils packed into his cupboards. She didn't know he liked to cook.

"Need a hand?" Theresa asked.

Meredith turned to her sister with a bright smile. "No thanks. Ash is always rearranging his stuff. Why didn't the kids want to come?"

"Teenagers," Theresa said with a shrug. "Too cool to hang with the parents."

"Still, it's a shame Dave had to stay behind to

keep an eye on them."

"He's not much of one for dinner parties anyway." She slanted Meredith a look that was all too familiar from their childhood. "Asher seems nice. We all wondered if he might have been a figment of your imagination when you never brought him home."

"Sounds like something you'd dream up," Meredith said through clenched teeth. "Maybe I just didn't want to scare him off. Did you ever think about that? This group, en masse, is a lot to cope with when you're not used to us."

"Asher has three sisters. I'm pretty sure he can handle us."

Three sisters! She hadn't known that about him, either. When Asher wasn't on one of his countless dates they hung out surfing sometimes, but never discussed their families. Which maybe stemmed from her not wanting to bring up the topic.

"Dave ran into Zack at the gym last month," Theresa said casually. "Did you know he's getting married?"

17

Theresa was loving this!

Meredith kept her face expressionless. "Why would I?"

You were engaged to the guy," Theresa said.

"Luckily, I realized it was a mistake before it was too late." *Unlike you.*

Not that Theresa would ever admit her marriage had been a mistake, but Meredith knew why Dave was happy to stay behind at the resort instead of having dinner with the family.

Theresa narrowed her gaze in that way Meredith remembered detesting during their childhood. "You left that one awfully close to the wire before you pulled the plug."

Meredith pulled a stack of plates from the cupboard and banged them onto the counter, harder than necessary. "Can we please talk about something else?"

"No need to get violent with the tableware," Theresa said, as if the fault lay with her. Her sister was a master at manipulation. "We're just all happy you finally met someone else."

She said *finally* as if it had been forever. How long since she had started mentioning Asher in her emails and Facetime? When had she first sent her mom pictures of the two of them together?

She shoved a handful of forks and napkins into her sister's hand. "Take these out to Asher, would you?"

By the time she returned to the lanai, Asher was deep in a 'boy chat' with her father and Michael. Her dad gave her an approving smile as she passed him to set the plates on the table.

"Great guy you've got here, sweetheart. He's offered to take us fellas fishing while we're visiting." He lowered his voice. "I hope you don't mind the way we just kind of barged in on you. You know what your mother's like when she takes a notion."

"I can hear you," Helen sang out from the other side of the lanai.

"What did I say?" Bill challenged her.

"Doesn't matter. My ears are burning," Helen said.

19

Asher stepped forward and placed a platter with the fresh fish and grilled pineapple on the table. "Help yourselves, everyone. Don't let it get cold."

"What's this stuff?" Emily wrinkled her nose as she pointed to the dish of poke.

"My specialty." Asher flashed his trademark smile and Meredith watched her youngest sister melt. He was a charmer, all right, and he knew how to work it. Now to survive the next week.

* * *

Something interesting was going on between Meredith and her family, but Asher couldn't quite put his finger on what it was. Her mom, soft and blonde, could easily stand in for most TV sitcom moms. Yet she cast more than a few worried looks Mer's way when her daughter's attention was elsewhere; a frown that instantly turned into a delighted smile if Meredith looked her way.

"The weather is wonderful here," Helen gushed. "I see now why you decided to move."

"There were a lot of factors in my decision," Meredith said.

Helen's smile faded.

Asher slung an arm across her shoulders. "I thought you came here to surf. Meeting a hot guy like me was just a bonus."

Privately, he figured she moved here to get away from her nosy family, but that was just his take. Being the baby among his own siblings, he'd had to train his older sisters not to helicopter him. Luckily, they all had their own kids now to torture. Still, he missed everyone like crazy and went home to Florida as often as he could. As far as he knew Mer never went home, which made it hard to fault this crew for taking matters into their own hands and springing a visit.

Also, as far as he knew, Mer hadn't been on a single date in the entire three years since she arrived. Which meant there was more to the story. And high time he found out what.

Eventually the time change caught up and the family said their good nights, leaving him and Meredith alone with the dishes.

"I got this," he told her.

She set her mouth in that stubborn way. "You cooked for my family. I'm not about to bail and leave you with the mess."

He chucked her an apron. "Have it your way." He pulled a quarter from his pocket. "Heads you wash, tails I dry."

"Is the machine just for show?" she asked.

"Nah," he said. "I use it all the time. But I thought it would be cute to see you in the dishpan, up to your elbow in suds."

Meredith gave him an eyeroll and opened the dishwasher. "How about I scrape and rinse, you load?"

"It's only equitable labor if you stick around and help to put away after they're done."

"You drive a tough bargain," Meredith said. "Do you compost?"

He leaned in close enough to catch a whiff of the light, floral scent she wore. Perfume and cologne were off-limits at work, so her fragrance choice was a nice glimpse into what made her tick, something he'd been trying to figure out since they first met. "Don't you think that's something you ought to know about me, seeing as how we're talking about tying the knot?"

She blew out a breath that stirred the hair on her forehead. "You don't have to do this, Ash."

"Maybe I want to," he said cockily. "Get to know your family; maybe I'll also get to know you."

"Trust me, you know as much as you want to know."

"You have a secret or two." He liked what was happening here. Her in his kitchen, the two of them bantering as they did the dishes and wiped the counters; he could almost believe the role he'd been cast in.

"And you don't?"

She had him there. It wasn't so much a secret; just something he didn't go around broadcasting. "Men are like onions," he said smugly. "You need to peel back our layers and find out what's in the center."

"In my experience, one layer is pretty much the

same as the last. For that matter, I don't even like onions."

"Blasphemy!" he said in mock horror.

"It's true. I pick them off my burger."

He pretended to shudder. "Who does that?" He moved closer. "I admit I noticed that about you. No onion breath. Just like now. Pineapple sweet."

He knew he was pushing her comfort zone. Mer was one of those people who always had an invisible line drawn around her, keeping people at arm's length. She'd been that way toward him from the beginning, and it took a while before he'd manage to creep under the wire as her "buddy". At first, he'd been comfortable in the role. Until he wasn't.

"I like your dad. Good guy. A little overwhelmed by all the women in his life."

"That's how you two connected," she said with a slow-dawning smile that sent his insides into a flurry.

"It was definitely a bonding moment," he said. "I expect there will be others this week ahead."

She sent him a look. "You're really going through with this? Hang out with my fam and pretend we're a couple."

"Sure. Why not?"

"Just as long as we're clear. Before they leave, you have to break up with me."

Chapter 3

"Why do I have to be the bad guy? Why can't you break up with me?" Asher said.

Meredith felt her heart start to race. "Trust me on this. I can't end things between us." If she did that, rejected Asher who they obviously had taken a shine to already, she would never hear the end of it. It's not that she was a commitment-phobe. She loved weddings. Other peoples' weddings. She admired the couples who trusted her to make their special day even more special. But how did anyone really know for certain that this was the one person they were fated to spend the rest of their life with?

She'd rushed into things with Zack, basking in her family's approval as she made plans to finally settle down. Until one day, shortly before their wedding, it happened all over again. She woke up covered in hives and unable to speak. She felt like she was drowning.

Cowardly, she knew, but she broke up with

Zack in a text, canceled the church, the caterers, the florist, the photographer by email, and fled town, taking refuge on a nearby island, some place she'd never been before where no one would look for her.

She looked up to see Asher's probing gaze, as if he was trying to peel back her skin and pry into her inner workings.

"What if I don't want to end things between us?"

"What do you mean? There are no 'things' between us."

He nudged closer, his hip brushing hers, his gorgeous greenish blue eyes alight with an emotion she couldn't quite identify. "There is this week." And he kissed her.

Meredith froze. Asher couldn't kiss her. They were friends. A kiss would change everything. Maybe even ruin their friendship.

Except it felt nice. Reassuring and comforting, a sense of finally coming home after a long, lonely exile. Was kissing a friend supposed to feel like this? For there was nothing awkward in their embrace, as if their bodies knew each other well and had been waiting for this moment.

Her limbs softened, relaxed into him, welcoming his assured touch, from the way his hands sleeked her back and her hips, to the way his lips shaped themselves to hers, sending the blood coursing through her veins. She plowed her hands through the fullness of his hair, her fingertips loving the soft, wavy texture.

Her entire body sparked to life, reminding her it had been a long time since she had been held like this, and forever since she had shared such a kiss.

Her knees felt weak by the time the kiss ended. Luckily, Asher kept hold of her, giving her time to recover her equilibrium.

"Wow!" She kept her voice light, once she finally caught her breath. "You're good at that."

His lips quirked in a satisfied smile. "I'm happy you approve."

"No, really," she said. "No one will doubt your intentions once they see us lip-locked."

His hands were linked behind her, keeping their

bodies touchingly close. "Isn't that the idea?"

Bad idea!

"Believe me, when I started this charade, I never imagined for one second that they would just show up unannounced and put us both on the spot."

He continued to smile down at her. "But you told them I was your ideal man? You sent them photos of me? Of us?"

"I knew they wouldn't believe me without some sort of visual proof."

"Why is that?" He asked as if he truly meant it, truly cared about her family dynamics.

She wasn't falling for it. Asher had proven tonight that he was a gifted actor. Her entire family believed they were a couple.

Day by day, she told herself. Get through this week. If Asher wouldn't dump her publicly, she'd break the news to them once they left, that things were over. They'd worry that she was up to her old habits, but wouldn't be able to do anything about it.

"They're suspicious by nature," she said, pulling back from the comfort of his embrace.

"Much like you."

"I'm not suspicious. I take people at face value."

"Including all those women who throw themselves at you?" she said.

"It's part of my job to make sure the guests have a memorable time," he said. "Some women just need a little extra reassurance about their own self-worth."

Uh oh! She resembled that remark.

Believing the men when they told her they loved her. Yet once the ring was on her finger, it became obvious the words were just lip service. A way to keep her needing their reassurance that she was loveable.

"Is that why you made friends with me? In your eyes I'm a charity case."

He withdrew as well. "Obviously your family doesn't have an exclusive on questioning people's motives."

Meredith glanced around, feeling trapped. "How long before the dishwasher is finished it's cycle?"

His gaze on hers saw way too far below the surface. Saw things she didn't want him to see; her sudden panic exposed.

"No need for you to stick around. I'll see you tomorrow."

Meredith didn't need to be told a second time. She grabbed her purse and fled.

* * *

Asher loved puzzles. As a kid, he'd graduated from jigsaw puzzles to Rubik's cubes and beyond. Solving puzzles meant he competed solely with himself. A level playing field and all that. When he was older, he discovered that humans presented the biggest puzzle of all, and spent much of his time figuring out what made other people tick. What kind of questions to ask. How to interpret their reactions, because let's face it, most people showed you the person they thought you were expecting to see, keeping their inner truths and demons hidden.

He'd known from the start that Meredith's story would be an interesting one, and so far he hadn't been wrong.

He slid behind the wheel of his Jeep. "Asher, you handsome devil!" he told his reflection as he adjusted the rearview mirror. "It's showtime."

At the marina where he kept his boat, he loaded a cooler packed with beer and sandwiches before he cast off and headed for the resort where the Robb family would be waiting. At least he hoped they would be waiting. He checked his waterproof dive watch, aware he was punctual to a fault. If only the rest of the world operated the same way.

He spotted Meredith first. Maybe because he was programmed to seek her out in a crowd. Tall and willowy with dark brown hair, she stood apart from her mom and sisters, all of whom were short, curvy and fair. Everyone was in shorts except Meredith in a sunshine yellow sundress that showed off her long, tanned, surfer's legs.

The kids were nowhere in sight, thank goodness. They must be at the kids' club with others their own age. He liked his nieces and nephews in small doses, but they were young and easy to amuse. Teens—he still wished he could wipe his own teen years right off the map. He didn't know if he'd suffered more because his sisters defended him, or if those years would have been even worse without them.

It wasn't until the summer after high school that the magic happened. Almost overnight he grew a foot, his skin cleared up, his face took on a chiseled definition while his baby fat morphed into lean muscles and washboard abs. Suddenly, women flocked to him like bees to honey and he loved them all, young, old, and in between.

He pulled up to an empty slip at the dock. Meredith got there first and caught the line he threw her. "I thought we'd be going out in one of the resort boats."

"You ever think maybe the resort has them booked for the day?"

"I didn't think," Meredith muttered as she climbed on board and looked around. "I didn't know—is this yours?"

He placed his index finger on her lips,

caressing the softness. "Sshh. Let them assume we've been out together on my boat many times these past three years."

He turned and waved to Joel, who was herding a group of resort guests over to the boat used for snorkeling excursions. Joel immediately veered toward them.

"Look at you two, all cozy. That the family?" Joel said, watching them parade down the dock.

Asher instinctively curled his arm around Meredith's waist. "It is. Where you taking the gang?"

"Out to Kua Bay. Where are you headed?"

"I'm not sure yet. I'll see what the others want to do. I brought snorkeling gear as well as paddleboards." Just then the rest of the Robb family descended and Joel returned to his group. Asher saw Helen's approving smile when she spotted his arm around Meredith.

"Look at you two lovebirds," she cooed. "Together almost three years and you'd think it was your first date."

"Every day with this woman feels like the first," Asher said, puzzled by the way Helen seemed to thrive on seeing them as a couple, almost as if she didn't quite believe it. Reluctantly, he moved from Meredith's side to grab his guests' gear and give them a hand boarding. Once they were settled, he untied the boat, pulled in the fenders, then climbed up to the command bridge and started the engine.

Down below, Meredith and her family milled about on the main deck, phones out snapping photos as they pulled away from the resort.

Minutes later, Helen popped up and lowered herself into the seat next to his. "Meredith never mentioned that you own your own boat."

"No?" Asher scrambled for a plausible reason. "We don't use it as much as I'd like. Work schedules and all."

"Meredith never told me how you two met, exactly. All I know is that it happened at the resort."

Asher blanched. Clearly, they ought to have

got their stories lined up last night when they were doing the dishes, instead of flirting and kissing.

"That's Mer's story," he said smoothly. "Let's wait for her version."

"That's what I mean," Helen said. "There are two versions to every story."

Asher grinned. "Actually, it's three. His, hers, and the truth."

Helen tapped his forearm lightly. "That's why I'm asking for yours. Meredith always edits what she tells me."

"I do not!" Meredith joined them and passed her mother an acrylic beverage glass.

"Your mother is trying to get me to spill secrets," Asher told Meredith.

She turned to her mother. "Why would you think I'm keeping secrets?"

Helen rolled her eyes at Asher. "She was always a tight-lipped little thing, even as a toddler. Not at all like her sisters."

"That's because I couldn't get a word in edgewise around them."

"What else was she like when she was young?" Asher asked, deftly steering the conversation away from the two of them. "She's tight-lipped with me, too, you know."

"She was very intelligent," Helen said. "Too smart, really. I agreed to have her skip a grade at school and then always wondered if it was a mistake. Maybe it would have been better to leave her with her peer group."

Asher had always found intelligence damn sexy, one of the reasons he'd been drawn to Mer in the first place.

"I never really had a peer group," Meredith said. "I was taller than everyone else and they called me 'Giraffe'."

"I thought it was a cute nickname." Helen turned to him. "She wasn't at all outgoing the way her sisters were. The other two always had lots of friends around."

One more nugget which gave Asher new insight. He could just see Meredith on her own, tall and gangly with her nose in a book; nothing in common with her giggly sisters and their friends. These days she had a few friends among the staff, but no 'bestie' that he was aware of. When they hung together it was always just the two of them.

From below, he heard the merriment on the main deck. Someone had figured out the boat's music system, and the sisters were dancing and cavorting to some classic rock that was older than they were.

"Was it love at first sight with you two?" Helen asked.

Asher placed a hand on Meredith's knee. "It was for me. Mer was a bit of a hard sell, but eventually I wore her down."

"You were very tenacious," Meredith said. "Never taking 'no' for an answer."

"Good," Helen said approvingly. "Keep that up." She rose and took her drink to the deck below.

"Sorry about that," Meredith said. "I doubt she's finished grilling you yet."

"I can embellish with the best of them," Asher said. "I just don't want to say anything in direct contradiction to what you've told them about us."

Meredith stared up at the sky, where fluffy white clouds were pushed around by the trade winds. "I told them all the resort guests adore you, and that you I both enjoy surfing. That you're from Florida originally, and we both started work here around the same time."

"It was the same day," Asher said.

"Was it? I didn't remember that detail."

But he did!

He remembered thinking in their new staff orientation that she wasn't shy, just slightly aloof, a trait he found intriguing.

Ever since that magic summer when he was eighteen, women of all ages had thrown themselves at him nonstop. Meredith's lack of interest had been a refreshing change. Much as she pretended to be an untouchable ice princess, he had immediately seen beneath her chilly façade to her vulnerable underbelly and wondered what had led to her crusty outer shell. Finally, her family was giving him insights into what made her tick.

"Come here," he said. "Take the wheel for a bit."

"Oh, I couldn't," she said.

"Sure you could." He patted his knee. "I'll walk you through it. It's a good skill to have in case we're out here someday and I fall overboard."

After a brief hesitation, Meredith perched on his knee and placed her hands stiffly on the wheel. He slid his arms around her middle and placed his hands over hers. "See," he said. "Nothing to it." Unfortunately, he didn't get her to himself nearly long enough before the clan intruded.

"Nice boat," Bill said. "Must have set you back a few bucks?"

"She's a 1983 Trawler." Asher said. "An oldie but a goodie. I got a good deal when her owner died and the widow didn't want it. Plus, it needed a bit of work, which deterred any serious buyers."

Bill nodded and pulled on his beer. "I'd love to have a boat."

"I haven't been to the Pacific Northwest," Asher said, "but I understand there are lots of things to see and do from the water."

"Like here, only colder. What's that over there?" Bill pointed.

"Puoloa Point," Asher said. "One of hundreds of great places on the island to hike."

Theresa turned up her nose and he felt Meredith, still on his lap, tense up. He gave her back and shoulders a reassuring stroke with his free hand, letting her know she wasn't on her own with this bunch.

"We've got tons of great hiking spots in the Pacific Northwest," Theresa said. "I'd rather do something different while we're here."

"For now, I thought we'd just putter along the coastline for a bit, so you can get your bearings," Asher said. "Joel took the resort guests to Kua Bay, but they'll leave after lunch. It's a great snorkeling spot."

"As long as we're not back too late," Theresa said. "I don't want to leave the kids alone all day."

"Maybe you shouldn't micro manage them so much," Emily said.

"Easy to say when *you* don't have kids," Theresa said.

Asher watched Emily recoil from the remark, while Dave made a face behind Theresa's back. Interesting dynamics. Every family had them.

"Anyway, Michael and I want to go see the volcanos while we're here," Emily said. "I wasn't even born when Mt. St. Helens erupted."

Helen laughed. "All I remember is the mess. Ash covering everything, right Bill?" She didn't wait for her husband to answer. "I was hoping to see sea turtles hatching."

"We have the Hawksbill turtles here on the island," Ash said. "They're an endangered species that nest from May to October, so you're a bit late for hatching season. Meredith and I joined the volunteers last year to monitor the shoreline and close it off where the nests were."

Meredith shot him a grateful smile. Clearly, she remembered that time as well. "We stayed up all night, protecting the babies from predators," she said.

Asher smoothed back a strand of hair that had blown across her cheek and stuck there. "It was a really magical evening," he said huskily. One which left him hungry for more times like that with Meredith. "How about we drop anchor as we get close to Kikaua Point and jump in the water before lunch?"

Chapter 4

Meredith didn't think Asher intended for their excursion to turn into a sunset cruise, but it worked out that they pulled up to the slip at the resort just as the sun was going down. On shore, she heard the traditional blowing of the Conch shell. Before she could explain the traditional behind it, Asher took the lead and explained the legend far better than she ever could have.

She thought back to her first memory of Asher. The resort staff had all gone out after work to a local bar. She remembered how their eyes met across the room and her stomach did a giant somersault. His gaze never left hers as he started in her direction, only to be waylaid by a fellow coworker. Over the other woman's head his eyes held hers briefly before he quirked a brow and turned his attention to the woman in front of him.

And right then, she knew. Gorgeous, sexy Asher was a man who loved woman—all of them.

And she wasn't about to get sucked in. She'd been there before—nearly married one of his type. And she had no intention of going down that road again.

The next time they were out with the gang, she called him "pal" and "buddy" and set the boundaries. As the years passed, she came to consider him a friend, but still maintained the cool, aloof façade that helped keep her safe.

Theresa was the first one off the boat, not stopping to thank Asher for the tour. "Come on Dave. I told you we never should have left the kids alone all day. Their camp will have ended hours ago. Lord only knows what they might have gotten up to."

Dave rolled his eyes as he stopped to shake Asher's hand. "Thanks, Asher. We had a great time."

Up ahead on the dock, Theresa turned and glared at her husband, as if her look alone would hurry him along.

Dave's voice carried as he reached her side. "They'll be fine, dear. They're responsible teenagers, which you'd know if you ever gave them the chance to be independent."

"Are you joining us for dinner tonight?" Emily asked, as she and Michael prepared to disembark.

"Not tonight," Asher said. "I have to get the boat tucked in back at the Marina."

"Mer?" Emily said.

"You go ahead," Meredith said. "I'm just going to check on a couple of things in the office before I go home."

"I thought you had the week off," Helen said.

"Which I didn't know about in advance so I could plan accordingly," Meredith said pointedly. "I want to make sure my assistant isn't messing things up."

Helen shot Asher a look. "She always was a control freak. Lists and more lists. Lists of her lists." She turned to Meredith. "You ought to lighten up a bit. Go with the flow the way Asher does. He's not in a tizzy because he didn't know we were coming."

He also didn't have a power-hungry assistant

47

with her eye on his job. Chloe's attempts to undermine her might be subtle, but Meredith knew the younger woman was ambitious to a fault. And resented Meredith as her boss.

At last they were gone. Meredith breathed a sigh of relief as she turned to Asher.

"That wasn't so bad. One day down, six to go," he said cheerfully.

"Five and a half too many," Meredith said.

He put his hands on her shoulders and for once she didn't have the urge to pull away, to wrap her arms protectively around her middle. Instead, she moved closer and rested her head against his muscled chest. "You're a trooper," she said against the front of his T-shirt. He smelled good. Sunshine and subtly-scented sunblock mixed with fresh ocean air.

His arms slid around her protectively, holding her in a comforting, nonthreatening way. He seemed to know exactly what she needed before she knew it herself. "We'll get through it."

She tilted her head up to meet his gaze. "Why

are you doing this? Why are you going out of your way to help me?"

He pressed a light kiss to her forehead. "'Cause I'm just that kind of guy."

They stood like that for several long, lovely minutes, their hearts beating in tandem, and for one crazy second Meredith wished it was real. That *they* were real.

On the heels of that thought came a wave of panic. She pulled back so abruptly she tripped and Asher reached out to steady her.

"You okay?"

She nodded blindly.

His voice rang with concern. "What happened, Mer?"

She stared at the deck. "I don't know what you mean."

He grunted and crossed his arms over his chest. "We all have secrets, Mer. How about you tell me yours and I'll tell you mine?"

"It's not much of a secret. Chloe has done a few things lately to try and undermine me. Between

Christmas and a full slate of weddings between now and New Year's, this is a terrible time for me to be away from the office."

"What kind of stunts is she pulling?"

"So far it's just been little things. Like saying she'll pick up something I ordered for a wedding, then conveniently "forgetting" and leaving me scrambling at the last minute. Neglecting to pass on my messages."

"I'm glad you told me," Asher said. "Maybe I can help."

Meredith blew out a breath. "You've done enough already, putting up with my family. I need to handle Chloe on my own."

He eyed her in a way that made her feel he could see inside her, stripping away her protective layers one at a time. "You don't like accepting help, do you?"

She pressed her lips together. "No more than I like compromise."

"Is compromise a bad thing?" Asher asked.

"It is when it's been the basis of your entire

life."

"I'm listening."

Meredith gathered up her things before she said too much. "And I'm off to check on my assistant and see what's she's been up to while I played hooky."

The evening activities at the resort were in full swing, and she avoided the flickering tiki torches and lanterns illuminating the beach area where a local trio entertained the crowd while a nearby limbo contest was underway.

What a disastrous mess she'd created and dragged poor Asher into the middle of. Funny thing was, he didn't seem to mind. Whatever secret he harbored couldn't be anywhere near as potentially damaging as hers. Men like Asher took for granted that everyone led the same charmed life they did.

She reached the lobby and started up the staircase to the second floor executive offices, just as one of her brides came rushing up behind her.

"Meredith! I've been looking for you everywhere. Can we talk?"

"Sure, Lauren. Let's go into my office."

Meredith led the way and unlocked the door, relieved to see Chloe had left for the day and the outer office was deserted. She could only image the spin Chloe would put on things if her assistant saw her in the company of a distressed bride. "Come on in here and we can talk." She indicated the love seat and headed for the seat next to it. "Would you like a bottle of water?"

Lauren crumpled onto the loveseat and shook her head, her eyes wide in her pale face.

"Is everything okay between you and Richard?" Meredith asked.

"I can't go through with it," Lauren whispered. "And I don't know what to do."

As she pushed a box of tissues closer to the woman, Meredith felt as if a huge hand grabbed her heart and squeezed. She'd only met Lauren and Richard and their parents a few days ago when they checked into the hotel. Before that, the wedding plans had been initiated by email and finalized through a Skype call.

The couple's wedding was nothing out of the ordinary. A simple beach front ceremony at sunset with a few dozen guests, followed by a buffet dinner and dancing on the lower terrace. The type of thing she had organized hundreds of times since she started working here.

She remembered Lauren being quiet through most of their conversations and figured the young woman was shy. Richard struck her as the take-charge type, a successful broker of high-end, luxury cars in a dealership started by his father. It wasn't the first time she'd seen a groom dominate the conversation.

Lauren's parents were a sweet, simple couple who had never been on a plane before and were clearly dazzled by the family their daughter was marrying into.

"You know, the way you're feeling right now is perfectly normal," Meredith said soothingly, even though her heart was pounding as if she'd just run half a marathon. "Suddenly getting cold feet is something I see with many of the brides who come through these doors."

"I can't be the type of wife his family expects me to be," Lauren whispered through pale, bloodless lips. "Originally, I thought if we really loved each other, we could overcome anything. We could make it work."

"Do you love him?" Meredith asked.

Lauren shredded a tissue between her fingers, then stared down at it, as if wondering how it got there. "I thought I did."

Boy, did that sound familiar!

"Did something happen?" Meredith asked.

"His best man got here earlier today," Lauren said.

"That's good," Meredith said.

Lauren continued as if she hadn't spoken. "And I saw—I saw the way they looked at each other. Richard never looked at me that way, not even once. His father saw it too. His face got all tight and angry and he dragged Richard off to his suite, which adjoins mine." At Meredith's questioning look, she flushed. "We haven't been together that way for quite a while—Richard said we should wait. I thought it was sweet, you know. Making our wedding night even more special. Anyway, I heard him and his father fighting."

Her hands shook, her chest rose and fell. "His father told Richard to do whatever he wants as long as he's discreet. But that he needs a wife for appearances sake. He said 'mousy Lauren' was perfect for the job. Hardly the type to cramp Richard's style or ask questions."

Meredith sat back in her seat. "What would you like to do?"

"I don't know," Lauren wailed. "What should I do?"

* * *

It was hours later when Meredith had things somewhat under control, with Lauren, along with her parents and friends, discreetly moved to a different resort on the other side of the island. One part of her brain followed the step-by-step protocols when a wedding is abruptly cancelled. Get hold of the florist, the catering and banquet staff, the musicians, and everyone else involved. Her fingers flew over the keyboard as she sent email after email.

Her final stop was Richard's suite to deliver the letter Lauren had written. Her heart pounded as she knocked on the door and waited. The past came flooding back bringing memories of canceling her own wedding with less than twenty-four hours' notice. The confusion and disappointment of not just Zack, but her own family, in what had started to look like a trend. Which was precisely where a lifetime of trying to please everyone but herself landed her.

When no one answered the door, she let out a sigh of relief. Richard was probably with his buddies at a stag off-site. She just hoped he was as relieved as Lauren that they weren't going through with a charade of a wedding simply to appease his parents.

Appeasing parents. Hadn't she done the same thing when she fabricated her relationship with Asher? Feeling she would never manage to live up to their expectations.

She bent down and slid the letter under the door. As she straightened and turned to leave, she saw a brief flash of movement near the corner at the end of the hall, like the swish of someone's skirt as they hurried out of sight. But no one had been in the elevator with her. She stared in that direction for several seconds before she turned away. It had been a long, stress-filled day. No doubt she was imagining things.

* * *

It took a while for Asher to get his boat cleaned up and tucked in for the night. Normally he found the ritual soothingly mindless as he secured the lines and turned off the engines before he rounded up used towels and empty bottles, but tonight as he battened things down his head buzzed from the day's activity and the dynamics of Meredith with her family. Clearly, there was a lot going on below the surface. One more puzzle for him to solve.

For a minute there on the boat, once her family left, he thought she might open up to him. Instead, she'd deftly changed the topic to her assistant, and he wasn't surprised when she turned down his offer to help. Not that he had any intention of just standing back. Things that mattered in Meredith's world affected him as well.

There were no lights on inside her condo when he drove past, convincing himself it was on his way home, or just about. At the end of the street, he turned around and drove back toward the hotel. It was unusual for any day staff to be working this late. Something must have come up.

He pulled up outside the hotel and tossed his keys to the valet. "Just checking on a couple of things, I won't be long."

Inside the lobby he saw Chloe, Meredith's assistant, slink down the staircase, cast a quick look around, and leave by the far door. So Chloe was working late as well. He started toward the stairs, wondering if she and Meredith had had words. Good thing he was here if Mer needed him.

He ran into her on the landing.

"Asher, what are you doing here?"

"Checking on you. Everything okay?"

He saw the way she hesitated before she nodded. "Just a couple of fires to put out. Nothing major."

He moved closer, feeling protective. "Your family?"

She gave her head a jerky shake. "More like a jittery bride. It's all handled."

He eyed her closely, certain there was more to the story than she was letting on.

"You eat yet?"

"I'm not really hungry."

"That's not what I asked." He looped an arm around her shoulder as they crossed the lobby. Her skin felt cold from more than the AC. "Lunch was a long time ago. And I have just the solution at my place."

"Really, Ash, I—"

"Remember how I don't take 'no' for an answer?" he teased. "Come on. My car's right out front."

Chapter 5

Meredith settled back in the passenger seat of Asher's Jeep, head against the headrest and closed her eyes, enjoying how nice it felt to have someone else take over for a change. The truth was, she was feeling fragile, first from deflecting subtle shots from her family all day, and then worrying about what Chloe was up to. Helping Lauren disentangle herself from what promised to be an awkward situation had stirred up a lot of raw edges around her own emotions.

It was past eight, but the air rushing by as Asher drove was balmy and warm, with that unique tropical scent that Meredith never got tired of.

"Frangipani," Asher said.

She started. "What?"

"You were wondering what that flower scent was."

"How did you know that?"

"Calculated guess that your senses are on high

alert from your recent adrenalin rush."

A chill grabbed hold of her heart and squeezed. "You can't know that about me."

"Sure I can. You were icy cold back at the hotel. Clearly, your system is running on empty. First up is to get some food into you and your blood sugar and equilibrium restored."

"I would have happily gone home and flopped into bed," she said.

"Worst thing for you," Asher said cheerfully. "You'd be awake in a couple of hours, unable to get back to sleep."

Meredith turned and stared out the window. There was a lot of truth in what Ash said. She hadn't been sleeping well lately, getting through the days on too much caffeine. When was the last time she'd taken an entire day to do something for herself, like go surfing?

Asher pulled to a stop in front of his house, turned off the engine and swung around to face her. "You okay?"

She opened her mouth to say yes, but the words

lodged in her throat. Instead, she found herself trussed up against Asher, soaking the front of his shirt with her sniffly tears. He held her tight, smoothing her hair with one hand as she let go of all the tension of the past forty-eight hours.

When she was all cried out, she pulled back, smiled self-consciously and swiped her cheeks with the back of one hand. "Sorry about that," she said. "I don't know what came over me. I never have a meltdown."

"I've been watching you for a while now. You've been pushing yourself pretty hard. Something was bound to give."

She nodded and let him help her out of the Jeep and into the house.

Once inside, he flicked on a few lights, turned on the oven and poured her a glass of wine. "Sip slowly," he said. "You need to get some food into you before you pass out."

"How come you're so good with hysterically sobbing females?" she asked.

"Three sisters," he said, as if that explained

63

everything. And maybe it did.

She perched on a stool at the island and watched as he heated and dished up leftovers from the meal last night.

"It's good," she said, after her first few bites.

"Always tastes better the next day."

Meredith didn't feel the need for small talk as she slowly unwound from the food, the company, and the wine. When he was done, Asher went back for seconds.

"Better?" he asked as he splashed a little more wine into her glass.

"Much." She pushed her plate aside, then watched him from beneath lowered lids as he rose and stacked their plates in the dishwasher. "You seem to have a gift for knowing and doing exactly the right thing at the right time."

"That's because we're in sync."

"We are?"

"Absolutely." He took her glass out of her hand and led her to the lanai. Once she was seated, he moved around behind her, pushed her hair aside and started to knead the tight muscles in her neck and shoulders.

"Keep that up, and you're never getting me to leave," she warned. She closed her eyes and concentrated on the sure yet gentle probing touch of his fingertips against her skin. Warmth from his touch radiated down her spine and a wave of relaxation followed. Her breathing grew shallow and her mind went blessedly blank.

"That was amazing," she said when he finished and took a seat next to her on the wicker settee.

"You're welcome."

It seemed natural to lean her head on his shoulder, for his arm to snake around her and snug her against him as they stared out into the night.

"Did you and your assistant have a confrontation tonight?" he asked.

"Nothing like that," Meredith said.

"But I saw—never mind," Asher said. "You were in your office a long time."

"I wasn't keeping track," she said, adding, "you were wonderful with my family, earlier."

"They're good people," Asher said. "And they obviously care about you."

"I know." She sighed. "It's just, some things can't be undone."

"Yeah, I get that," Asher said.

Somehow her free hand found its way to rest against the comforting muscular warmth of Asher's chest. She felt his fingers filter through her hair, and a slow, tingling warmth spread through her, thawing that lonely ice field deep inside. "What would you go back and change? If you could."

Asher's laugh was short and hollow. "How about the world's worst puberty?"

She made a disbelieving noise as she pulled back to study his expression. "Come on. I'm serious. It's obvious that you were born god's gift to women. I bet you were the tallest guy in the class, with all the girls in love with you. Captain of the Football Team and class valedictorian."

He gave her a long, searching look before he stood up. "Wait here." He was back a couple of minutes later and passed her his high school yearbook. It fell open to a page with the corner turned down.

Her eyes widened as she scanned the page. "Oh, no! Is this some kind of joke?" Her gaze met his. "They put the wrong person's picture next to your name."

"No, they didn't."

"But—"

"That was me back in high school. Short, fat, terrible skin, frizzy hair and glasses. No friends."

She looked from him to the photo and back to him. "I don't believe you."

"Meredith, this is not something a guy would make up."

"But you're—what happened?"

"How come I don't still look like that?" He gave a modest smile. "Suddenly, the gods smiled. I grew a foot, almost overnight which is not as cool as it sounds. It's actually quite painful. Bones stretching or whatever happens in a sudden growth spurt. Fat turned to muscle. My skin cleared up and my hair calmed down. I got Lasik surgery for my eyesight."

"And suddenly women found you irresistible."

He shrugged modestly. "So it would seem."

"Wow!" Meredith sat back. "That is quite the story. You must have had a lot of wild oats to sow, making up for lost time."

"I'm not like that, Mer. I genuinely enjoy women. I grew up in a house full of them. And in spite of, or maybe because of my past, I treat everyone nicely. It's not my fault that some people read more than they should into the fact that I am the proverbial nice guy."

He spread his hands flat overtop of the yearbook. "That's my ugly secret. What's yours?"

Meredith stiffened. "What makes you think I'm harboring a deep, dark secret?"

"I've seen the way your mother watches you when she thinks you're not looking. She worries about you more than the other two girls."

Meredith pressed her lips tightly together as she gathered her thoughts. "That jittery bride I mentioned earlier? Her story brought up a lot of things from my past."

"What kind of things?'

"Memories, emotions, doubts, pain."

His arm tightened around her. "That's a lot to pile on an already stressful day with your family."

"I've lost track of how many weddings I've planned over the years. The only number I'm clear on is four. Four weddings I've planned for myself. Four weddings I have not gone through with."

"Isn't there a movie about that?"

"*Runaway Bride*. It's actually a real thing."

"I was referring to *Four Weddings and a Funeral*." Asher gave his head a shake as if he was trying to figure it out. "What kind of a *thing* are you talking about?"

"The reason some brides run. The jury's out as to whether I'm a commitment-phobe, suffering from a lack of genuine love in my life, or have a fear of not living up to the expectations of others."

"I think you can rule out the 'lack of love' part."

"And I'm not afraid of commitment. I'm

committed to my job, my sport, my family."

"So committed to them that you made up a fake boyfriend so they wouldn't worry about you."

"It sounds silly when you put it like that."

"Nothing real is ever silly." He gave her a brotherly hug. "And you thought I left a string of broken hearts trailing behind me. What ever happened to your exes?"

"Most of them went on to marry a nice girl. The right girl for them."

"So, no harm, no foul."

One foul. One that was never far from mind.

"What happened tonight when you went back to the hotel?"

"My bride realized that she was about to make the biggest mistake of her life. I helped her escape before it was too late."

"Another runaway bride?"

"The poor girl suddenly realized her fiancée was more interested in his best man than in her. His parents knew the truth, but were pushing the marriage for appearance's sake."

"Will there be repercussions from the groom's family for the part you played?"

"Probably. If they decide to sue the hotel it could give Chloe the ammunition she needs to go after my job."

Asher nodded thoughtfully. "I admire you for doing the right thing and consequences be damned."

She snuggled against him, reassured by his support. "I hope it was the right thing."

Chapter 6

Asher's heart beat faster than normal as he held Meredith and inhaled the subtle smell of wildflowers or whatever scented the shampoo she used. Her hair was like silk beneath his chin, and she fit against him like she'd been created with him in mind.

He'd played this scene a million times in his mind, the two of them, cuddling and exchanging intimacies. Intimacies that took their friendship in an entirely new direction. When he pressed a light kiss to the top of her head, she turned her face his way. Kissably close.

Just one kiss. A teasing taste to slake his thirst and sustain him for whatever came next.

Her lips molded to his and her mouth opened, warm and pliant and hungry, a hunger that drove his own appetite to new dimensions. She moaned in the back of her throat and her arms cinched around his neck, holding him close. So close he never wanted to let go. When her body twined against his, the settee was suddenly cramped and restrictive. But he couldn't pull away. Her hands were everywhere, under his shirt, caressing his back, fondling his abs, while she pivoted her pelvis against his hip.

Her nipples hardened against the confines of her sun dress, begging for his touch, his tongue. He unfastened the buttons on the front of her dress and flipped open the front closure of her bra. Her breasts tumbled into his hands and she moaned aloud. Her breath caught on a sigh of delight as she squirmed against him.

He'd never known a woman to get so turned on so fast and his ego leapt to attention along with his cock, straining against the front of his board shorts. He took one delicious breast in his mouth and sucked greedily as she tunneled her hands through his hair and raked his scalp with her nails, all but bouncing up and down against his knee, her panties damp. She was shaking as much as he was by the time he disentangled himself enough to stand and scoop her into his arms.

"Bedroom," he said.

"I thought you'd never ask," she murmured, her lips warm against his neck as she tasted him.

The bedroom shutters were open and a swath of moonlight illuminated her features as he set her down gently, leaned over her and kissed her. He tried to go slow but she wasn't having it, ripping off his shirt and tugging down his shorts before she shrugged out of her dress and they were together, skin on skin.

Sudden uncertainty flickered across her face, and he paused. "You okay?"

She nodded and pulled him close. "Never better. I just wondered why this feels so right. And why we've never done it before."

Asher laughed. "Good question." And he proceeded to make up for the last three years.

* * *

Meredith woke up to find Asher watching her with a bemused look on his face. She started to sit up, tugging the sheet over her breasts and wishing she had a toothbrush in her purse. "What are you looking at?"

"You," he said. "You looked so content while you slept, and you made the most adorable little noises."

She slapped a hand against her mouth. "Please don't tell me I snore."

"It's more like the purr of a contented kitten."

"Hmm." It had been a long time since she'd had to navigate the awkward 'morning after' the first time. Hopefully Asher had the moves down pat and she could take her lead from him.

"Stay there, I'll go make coffee." She cast an admiring female glance as he padded from the room, magnificently naked. He really was a spectacular male specimen. So much so, it was difficult to reconcile the man she'd spent the night with and his high school photo. Did that insecure, chubby and friendless youngster ever creep unexpectedly into his psyche?

The second he was out the bedroom door, she raced for the bathroom.

She was barely back in bed before he returned with two steaming mugs. He handed one to her and slid in next to her, punching his pillows into a bolster behind his back as she took a grateful sip. Asher knew how she liked her coffee. Now he knew a whole lot of other things she liked as well.

"How did you get into surfing?" she asked. It seemed an interesting choice of sports for someone who hadn't looked exactly lithe and agile in their youth.

"A boyfriend of one of my sisters. I guess he felt sorry for me. He was a patient teacher and surprisingly, I had an aptitude for it. Team sports had never interested me, but out there on the water you're only competing against yourself and mother nature."

"You're lucky you could learn without a wet suit," she said, thinking back on her initiation to surfing in the chilly Pacific Northwest waters. One of her friends, Alisha, ran a surf camp on an island near where she lived.

"I don't know if they make them in 'husky

size'', he said. "I wore a 2XL rash guard to try and hide my blubber belly. Not that anyone was fooled once my rashie got wet."

She rolled over on her side, and ran a hand down his washboard stomach. "Do you ever worry you might suddenly get fat again?"

"Every day," he said.

She blinked, touched by his honesty. "How do you deal with that fear?"

He shrugged. "How does anyone deal with fear? They face it head on. Are you afraid you might not ever be able to follow through on a romantic relationship?"

She nodded. "I don't want to hurt anyone else. That's why I avoid entanglements."

"Hey," he said, "since we're officially off work, do you want to go surfing today?"

Before she had a chance to answer, there was a loud pounding on the front door.

Asher leapt up and into a pair of board shorts so fast his movements were a blur. Clearly, he'd had his post coital snuggles interrupted before.

She settled back with her coffee mug, wondering if this was the beginning of a regrettable entanglement, or if Asher simply wanted a fuck buddy.

What did she want it to be?

Her thoughts were interrupted by a babble of voices from the other room. *Oh no! They'd hunted her down!*

Reluctantly she got out of bed and picked up yesterday's rumpled dress from the floor, aware the significance of her attire wouldn't go unnoticed by her nosy family members. Her mother looked up as she joined Asher and her parents.

"You weren't answering your phone and you weren't at home," Helen gushed, "so we figured this was the only other place you could be."

Her dad gave her an apologetic look.

"The girls booked us pedicures at the hotel spa today, leaving the men free to go off and do some boy stuff."

Meredith ran a hand through her rumpled hair. "Asher and I were planning to go surfing."

"You two lovebirds can surf anytime," her mother said. "How often do you get to spend Christmas Eve day with your mom and your sisters?"

Very seldom, and mostly by design.

"Think of your presence as your Christmas present to each of us."

Meredith slapped her temple with the flat of her hand. "I already mailed your gifts to the house." Gift cards, actually, since she had no idea what any of them wanted or needed.

"That's okay, dear. This way we'll have something to open when we get back home."

"I need to stop at home and get changed first," Meredith said, knowing when she was beat.

"That's fine. We'll stay here and get to know Asher better while you do that. Like I said before, I don't know why you're paying two mortgages when it would be so much cheaper to live together."

Meredith figured she'd leave Asher to respond to that one.

"Now, Helen," he said. "You know how

independent Meredith can be."

Meredith was out the door before she realized she didn't have her car here. Oh, well. The walk would do her good. Give her a chance to clear her head after her night with Asher.

* * *

Asher mentally congratulated himself on the way he rebounded with the arrival of Meredith's parents. On the one hand, he'd been looking forward to spending the day together, just the two of them. On the other hand, he didn't want Meredith to feel crowded and bolt, so maybe a little breathing room was what she needed.

Not that she'd get much chance to breathe around her family. He could tell Helen's love and concern for her daughter was genuine. But hadn't she figured out by now that the bulldozer approach was all wrong where Mer was concerned?

Hell, *he* wasn't even sure what the right approach was. And as he and Meredith's dad made plans for a golf day with Meredith's two brothers-in-law, he hoped to have a few more insights by the end of the day. He knew there had to be more to the runaway bride story than she had shared last night.

The resort boasted a Jack Nicklaus Championship course with lava contours interrupting the green, the last holes of the seven-acre stretch ending at the ocean. The most popular course on the island, it was always heavily booked but Asher used his charm and contacts to secure them a tee-time, then arranged to rent clubs and carts. He just hoped Meredith's family members had proper shirts and tailored shorts.

He and Bill drove back to the resort together as Meredith and her mom had gone ahead in the rental car. The girls' spa date had an earlier booking time than their tee time. Which is how he found himself enjoying a late breakfast/early lunch with Bill, Dave and Michael.

"How are your kids enjoying themselves?" he asked Dave, after their round of beer had been served.

"They're having a blast," Dave said. "Thriving in the absence of their helicopter mother, for sure."

"I've noticed kids today don't seem to have anywhere near the freedom we did at their age," Asher said.

"Theresa acts like there's a predator lurking around every corner. I don't know how she expects them to gain any street smarts when she's controlling their every move. Or trying to."

"I can't really speak to that," Asher said. "Not having kids of my own."

"Me either," Michael said. "Emily and I are on the fence if we're ever going to have any. Have you and Meredith talked about it?"

Asher's collar felt a little tight. "It seems a little premature."

"Take my advice," Dave piped up. "Don't wait till it's too late to figure out you have different ideas about pretty much everything."

Interesting comment. Just then, their server arrived with four food plates balanced perfectly. He pushed his beer aside to make room for his lunch.

"Of course," Dave said as he picked up his burger, "odds are against Meredith showing up on the big day if things go that far. Given her track record, I mean."

"Dave," Bill said with a warning tone.

"It's okay," Asher said. "I know all about Meredith's issues with commitment and follow through."

Next to him, Bill gave a sigh of relief. "I'm glad she told you."

"Me, too," Asher said, and meant it. He was keen to learn everything he could about Meredith and what made her tick.

They were on their way to the clubhouse when Asher ran into Joel.

"You go ahead," he said to the others as he flagged down his helper. "I'll be right there."

"How's it going?" Joel said. "You guys engaged yet?"

"Depends if you'll be my best man or not." Asher punched his arm. "Seriously, I need a favor. You know Meredith's assistant, Chloe?"

"The exotic-looking broad? A bit. Why?"

"See if you can strike up a friendship with her.

Meredith's expecting a knife in her back one of these days. Pretend you're going after my job. Maybe you can get her to open up as to what she's got up her sleeve."

"You know I'd never do that to *you*, right?" Joel said.

"I know, bro. But having grown up with three sisters, I also know it's different for women trying to get ahead. Some of them have few qualms about changing the rules or playing dirty if they feel it's justified."

Joel gave a lascivious grin. "Maybe I can get Chloe to play dirty with me."

"Pervert."

Joel shrugged. "If the end justify the means—"

Chapter 7

As Meredith took a seat in the pedicure station, which was laid out with four reclining chairs in a row, each one fronted by an attendant's stool, she felt guilty for counting the days until her mother and sisters cleared off back to Seattle. They meant well. She might as well try to relax and enjoy their company as her feet soaked in the warm, fragrant foot bath provided by the attendant. She reached for her champagne flute just as her mother ruined the mood.

"Have you met Asher's family yet, dear?"

"Not yet," Meredith said into her glass, before taking an extra big swallow.

"Surely you've Facetimed or Zoomed with them," Helen said, displaying a level of techno-savvy Meredith didn't know her mother possessed. Mostly the two of them emailed or texted.

"No, Mom. We've been keeping things pretty much to ourselves. Especially here at work."

"I would, too, if I was you," Theresa said snidely. "I mean given what you do, planning other people's weddings, and what's gone down in the past."

Meredith bit her lip. No point engaging with her sister's barbed comments. Which were another thing she hadn't missed in the past three years.

"I ran into your little assistant at the hotel earlier," Theresa continued. "Sweet gal."

"She's okay," Meredith said noncommittally.

"She thinks a lot of you." Theresa frowned at her fingernails as she spoke. "She was most complimentary, telling me how much she's learned from you. And how excited she is to be in charge while you're off this week."

I bet she is.

"Now, Theresa, Meredith doesn't want to talk about work," Helen said, turning her attention back to Meredith. "How many nieces and nephews does Asher have?"

Work was a far safer topic than this.

"Five or six," she said vaguely, as the attendant

lifted her feet from the water and dried them off. Sounded like a safe enough guess.

"Once you and Asher set a date, I hope it's all right if I give his mother a call. Get to know her a bit before the wedding."

"Mom, please don't rush things, okay? I promise you'll be the first to know anything important."

"I hope so." Helen looked hurt. "Asher said he goes home to Florida several times a year. I'm surprised you've never gone with him to meet everyone."

"Why would she?" Emily looked up from the fashion magazine she was paging through. "She never comes to see us."

"I told you, things with Asher and I are very much on the DL for now," Meredith said. "As for coming home, my schedule just hasn't fit in with yours."

"You know we'd always make time," Helen said.

Meredith reached over and patted her mother's

hand. "I know, Mom. I've just had some things to work out. That's all."

Her mother nodded. Meredith knew Helen was remembering the aftermath of her last break-up—and the reason she'd moved as far away from Seattle as possible.

"It was nice of Asher to take the boys golfing today. Is he a good golfer?"

"Asher's good at everything," Meredith said noncommittally. *And a little too good at being a fake boyfriend.*

* * *

By the time they reconvened with the male half of their group, she learned that Asher had invited everyone for a Christmas day picnic on the beach.

"Are you sure that's a good idea?" she whispered to him.

Asher shrugged. "They're not going away. They want to spend Christmas with us, so might as well show them how we do things here." He gave her a quick, reassuring squeeze. "It'll be fine. Believe me, it's easier to be patient when it's not *my* folks."

* * *

Christmas Eve at the resort was packed with activities for all ages, including a visit from Santa for the younger children.

"You okay?" Asher asked, as everyone grabbed seats to watch a musical Christmas play in the amphitheater.

"It's a little weird for me to be on this side of the action" Weird was an understatement. Several times this evening she'd caught sight of Chloe hustling around behind the scenes and she actually felt a pang, wishing she was back there doing her job instead of playacting for her family.

"Let's see your toes," Asher said.

She raised one sandaled foot to show off her shiny magenta polish.

"Very nice." He caught her foot in one hand and gave it a teasing tickle. "Soft." Then he put his arm around her, a move that was starting to feel shockingly natural when they were around her folks.

She gave him a suspicious look. "What kind of guy cares about the color of a girl's nail polish?"

"A man who appreciates women."

And wasn't Asher's appreciation for the fairer sex one of the first things she'd noticed about him, after his killer body and sexy smile.

"How did things get so complicated?" she whispered as the action on stage commenced.

"When hasn't life been complicated?" he said.

Good point. Meredith tried to concentrate on the play.

Which wasn't easy snugged up against Asher with his familiar light, woodsy citrus fragrance wafting her way in the balmy evening air. Was it only this morning that she'd woken up in his arms? It felt like a lifetime ago.

And now she knew, firsthand, how it felt to be one of the many women appreciated by Asher. Even though he showed up to staff parties and events with a different woman every time, he always treated his date attentively, making sure they were having a good time and meeting other members of the team.

That's when she pegged him as the type of guy who wasn't meant to settle down. She'd met a few other men like him over the years who were pretty much considered public property, to be freely shared among the female population. The man knew it, and the woman accepted her time with him for what it was worth.

The lucky female, on her turn, got to bask in the man's undivided attention for a short while, knowing it would soon be time to pass him on to the next fortunate partner. With no intention in joining that camp, Meredith had opted for Asher's friendship instead, guaranteeing neither of them would get involved or get hurt.

So what happened?

Nothing happened! She and Asher were friends, that was all.

So why did she have this overwhelming urge to kiss her friend? To spend another night in his bed?

She glanced his way in the dark, pretty sure he would be agreeable to the idea, one she knew would be a mistake.

"I'm going to light out of here right after the show ends," she said. "Try and lose everybody in the crowd."

"Do you think that's wise?" Asher asked. "They'll probably wonder what's up."

"Call it self-preservation."

"You don't have your car here," Asher said. "I'll drive you home."

They were walking across the staff parking lot, headed for Asher's Jeep, when Meredith saw Chloe on the other side of the lot, getting into a car with a man. As the passenger door opened, the overhead light illuminated the couple inside.

"I didn't know Chloe and Joel were hanging out," she said when they reached the Jeep.

"Christmas tends to trigger lots of emotions," Asher said. "Maybe the two of them are just lonely and spending the holiday together."

Lonely! She knew all about that. And it was a feeling that always seemed worse when there were a lot of people around.

* * *

Meredith woke early Christmas morning from force of habit and started to jump up, when she remembered she didn't have to work today, and flopped back against the pillows. Chloe would be in attendance early, making sure the guests' stockings got distributed on time and *Breakfast with Santa* was under control. While Meredith got to endure a picnic with her family.

Picnic!

That thought catapulted her out of bed and into action. She hadn't prepared a single thing, and the stores were closed. What had Asher been thinking?

She raced over to his place a short time later, her hair still wet from the shower. He was in the driveway, his Jeep already loaded with a folding banquet table, folding chairs and a portable barbeque. Two big coolers were on the driveway next to his vehicle.

He saw her and made his way to where she parked; heartbreakingly handsome in a way that turned her insides to mush as he helped her out.

"Merry Christmas!" He gave her a light kiss on the lips that whetted her appetite for more. "Did you sleep okay?"

"I did until I woke up in a panic, worried about the picnic."

He trailed his fingers lightly up her bare arm. "You worry too much. I've got this."

"Ash—"

He kissed her again, for real this time, and she forgot what she was going to say.

"I can't let you do everything!"

He tilted his head and studied her, genuinely puzzled. "Why not?"

"It's not right. It's—"

"I wouldn't do this if I didn't truly want to show your family a good time."

She relaxed and sagged against him, grateful for his presence. "Why are you so good to me?"

"Beats me," he said with a grin. "You must be growing on me."

"What have you got going on?"

He waved a hand in the direction of his loaded

vehicle. "I went to the resort earlier and borrowed a few things the catering department didn't need today. We need an early start to get set up, or all the good spots will be taken. I'm running out of room, so how about I load the coolers into your car and you can follow me."

"I feel guilty. I didn't do a thing to help."

"You can help me load the surfboards."

"Are we surfing? I didn't bring my board."

He pointed to a board bag, standing apart from all the others. "Merry Christmas!"

She looked from him to the bag and back to him. "We never get each other gifts."

"You told me you had your eye on a new board."

Her heart raced as she bent to unzip the bag. Nestled inside was the stunning, vintage Dick Brewer board she'd been eyeing in the surf shop.

She reverently traced the master carver's logo, circled by a lei, before she straightened and turned to him. "How did you know this was the one? Last time I was in there, they told me it had been sold."

Asher smiled smugly. "I met Dick once, over on Kaui. He's an inspiration to shapers everywhere. You have excellent taste."

"I can't accept it," Meredith said flatly.

"Sure you can. I've watched you out there. This board has your name all over it."

Meredith swallowed thickly. Asher was right! She *was* good enough to ride this board. Why did it take him to drive the point home?

Chapter 8

Asher enjoyed surprising Meredith. She was so cute when she was flustered. He checked in his rearview mirror to make sure she was still behind him, reflecting on how good it felt to take some of the load off her shoulders these last few days. He wasn't sure why, but he had a feeling she would have found it a lot to be on her own with her family.

"Happy to help," he said aloud.

At that moment his phone rang, his blue tooth displaying Joel's number. "Merry Christmas." He hoped there wasn't some disaster at the resort that he'd need to deal with. He hadn't been on a Christmas picnic since he left Florida and was looking forward to it.

"Same to you," Joel said. "Listen I've been hanging with that Chloe broad the past day or so, she's pretty whacked."

Asher's hands tightened on the wheel. "In what way?"

"For starters, she's totally pissed at getting passed over for the director's job that Meredith has."

"I suspected as much. Mer said she's been doing some subtle undermining."

"Forget subtle," Joel said. "She's bringing out the big guns. Did you know Meredith has a track record of leaving her intended grooms-plural- at the altar?"

"I heard something about that."

"Well, Chloe's all over it. Once she has enough ammo, I guarantee she'll be taking it to the higher-ups to try and discredit Mer."

"Good work, buddy," Asher said. "Thanks for the heads up."

He pulled into the beach park and secured a primo spot where it was easy to unload and set things up a short distance from the shore. Meredith pulled in close behind him.

"This is perfect," she said.

"Yeah," Asher said with only half his attention, as he pulled out the light weight shade shelter and started to set it up.

"It looks like you thought of everything," Meredith said once their vehicles were unloaded, the table and chairs unfolded and in place, snacks laid out on the table and the portable barbeque set up and ready to go. A short distance away, on the closest patch of sand, stood the volleyball net they had put up. "I feel terrible that I didn't help. I mean, I'm an event planner for heaven's sake. I should have—"

"What? Made a couple dozen lists and stayed up all night making special Christmas napkin holders and place cards?"

Meredith lobbed the volleyball at him. "I'm detail-oriented. It goes with the territory."

He caught the ball easily. "I agree it can be an asset in a job like yours. But it can be a detriment in day-to-day life."

"Says Mr. Seat-of-his pants."

He flashed her a grin. "Anything my slap-happy-self forgot?"

"Nothing I've noticed yet. But the day is

early."

He pulled her to him. "Let it go, Mer." He smiled down at her, pleasantly surprised when she didn't pull away.

"I'm still overwhelmed by that board you bought me."

He fiddled with the ends of her pony tail. "I can't wait to see you ride it."

Her eyes were serious on his. "I wish—"

Whatever she had been about to say was drowned out by the loud honking of the resort shuttle as it pulled up and discharged the Robb family, including Santa Bill, sporting a Santa hat and a red sack.

Christmas greetings and hugs were exchanged all around and teams were picked to play volleyball before it got too hot. The two teenagers, Connor and Katie, whose fair skin had turned pink during their stay, feigned that bored, indifferent look of youngsters trying to pretend they were too cool for the proceedings or to be excited about Christmas, so Asher picked them both for his team. Helen opted to referee, which Asher took to be her way of keeping a mother hen lookout from the sidelines.

Bill, the opposing team captain, moved fairly quickly for a man his age. Theresa played across from Dave as if her life depended on winning. Emily and Michael were a study in team work, with her setting things up and him going in for the kill. Along with keeping an eye on his team, Asher felt Meredith's happy gratitude toward him every time he looked her way. Which meant everything he'd done to get ready for today had been worth it.

The tie-breaking third game came to an end abruptly when Theresa landed wrong on her ankle in the sand and went down with a cry of pain. Asher and Dave reached her at the same time. Asher stepped back to let Dave look after his wife while he went for an ice pack.

On his way to the cooler, he threw Meredith his keys. "First aid kit's under the driver's seat."

Theresa ignored her husband when Asher approached with the ice. "I don't think it's broken, do you, Asher?" Which meant he had little choice but to kneel at her side and gently examine her ankle.

Dave pulled back. "I think it's just sprained, hon."

Theresa ignored him to blink up at Asher. "I bet you have your first aid ticket."

"I do," he said as he made a thorough examination of her injury. "I agree with Dave. Let's get you into the shade and get some ice on it."

Asher looked over his shoulder to where Dave watched, his face unreadable.

"You want to give her a hand into the shade, Dave?"

Before Dave could reach them, Theresa grabbed onto Asher's shoulder in an attempt to hoist herself to her feet, leaving him no choice but to help her up.

"Should I go for an X-ray to be on the safe side?"

"I don't think that's necessary," Asher said, relieved when Meredith arrived with the first-aid kit.

Between him and Meredith, as Helen clucked in the background, they got Theresa settled with her injured ankle propped on a towel on a second chair and the ice in place.

"Dave, watch the kids," Theresa snapped. "I don't want them wandering off."

"It's all families here," Asher said. "Maybe they'll make some new friends."

First aid duties over, Asher opened a beer and fired up the barbeque while Bill distributed Christmas gifts to the family, and Theresa continued to bark orders from her makeshift throne. Asher could tell she wasn't enjoying this latest turn of events.

Meredith sidled up to him and helped herself to his beer, taking a long swallow before she passed it back. "You're a saint."

He tucked a flyaway strand of escaping hair behind her ear. "And now I know why you moved away from Seattle. Is your big sister always like that?"

"Bossy drama queen? Pretty much."

They were interrupted by Bill's "Ho, ho, ho", as he extended a brightly wrapped package to each of them before making his way to the others.

Asher stared down at the snowman covered wrapping paper. "I wasn't expecting a gift," he said to Meredith.

"Neither was I," she said, in a way that he knew she was referring to the surf board he'd given her earlier.

Asher ripped the paper off his present, which was a wooden gift box with a picture of a fish on the front. "Wow!" he said. "Smoked salmon." His gaze caught Helen and Bill. "Thank you, everyone. This is a treat."

"I hoped you like fish," Helen said with a pleased smile. "And this is something you can't get around here."

Asher looked at Meredith. "Aren't you going to open yours?"

"I guess," she said reluctantly, before she started to pick at the tape on one corner. Behind him, he heard Theresa telling her kids to pick up their gift wrap before it blew away.

"You too, Emily," Theresa called, which earned her a middle finger salute from her sister.

Meredith ripped away the Christmas wrap to reveal a shiny new photo album with the words *The Two of Us* etched on the cover.

"I know everyone has digital pictures these days," Helen said, "but I thought this might encourage you to print your favorites of the two of you to look back at over the years to come."

Wow. Subtle was not Helen's forte.

"Thanks, Mom."

He admired Meredith's brave smile as she made her way to her mother's side and hugged her.

"Who's getting hungry for a burger?" he called out.

"I don't eat red meat," Katie said disdainfully, twirling a strawberry blonde curl around her index finger.

"You need a little red meat from time to time," Theresa said, "or you'll become anemic."

Katie wrinkled her nose, which scrunched her

freckles.

"I brought some veggie burgers, just in case," Asher whispered to Katie, rewarded by a rare smile from the girl.

He turned to Meredith. "Do you mind grabbing me that pack of burgers out of the cooler?"

* * *

The day turned out better than Meredith anticipated. Asher and Dave took the kids paddle boarding after lunch, while Emily and Michael went off to explore the park. Even Theresa seemed to mellow out, and Meredith passed a pleasant hour or so with her parents and her sister, all of whom refrained from making any reference to upcoming engagements or weddings.

Despite that, she wasn't exactly sad when the shuttle showed up to collect the others and it was just her and Asher. As long as she could remember, a little time with her family went a long way. It felt completely natural to stand alongside Asher as they waved goodbye, his arm settled comfortably around her waist.

It felt even more natural to turn in his embrace and loop her arms around his middle like they were a real couple. She caught her breath at the look in his eye, an intimate look reserved for someone special. She reacted by trying to grab hold of a nonexistent love handle.

"I can't believe you used to be chubby," she said teasingly.

He gripped her hand in his. "Don't do that, Mer."

"Don't do what?"

"You know what. Try and deflect what's happening here. Pretend you aren't feeling what I feel."

She moved away, suddenly restless. "I feel hot. Worn out and relieved today is over and there are only a few more days before they're out of here for good."

"You'll miss them when they're gone."

She pushed away her thoughts. More than that, she'd miss Asher when he was no longer her fake boyfriend.

"Say we'll always be friends," she blurted out. "No matter what."

"Bff's," he said. "That I can promise. Pinkie swear."

Suddenly feeling lighter of heart than she had in a long time, maybe forever, Meredith helped pack up their belongings and load everything in their vehicles.

By the time she pulled up behind Asher at his place, her lighthearted mood had shifted gears to some place more serious. Asher had put her new surfboard inside for safe-keeping, and she didn't know what would happen next as she grabbed a cooler and followed him inside. She didn't know what she wanted except she didn't want to go home. Didn't want to be alone at Christmas.

Chapter 9

She'd only been to his house a few times, but tonight the interior felt warm and welcoming in a way her place never did. Asher turned on the Christmas lights in the house and on the lanai, and they worked in companionable silence unloading the coolers and putting things away. Instinctively she knew exactly where most things went, almost as if she'd been doing this for years.

When they were done Asher turned on some soft, soothing jazz, and poured her a glass of wine before he took her hand and led her to the couch.

"'Thank you' sounds so inadequate for everything you did today," she said, grateful for his comforting presence as he sat next to her. "I could have never made it through this week without you."

He rubbed a piece of her hair between his fingers in an intimate fashion as he gazed into her eyes. "I was happy to help."

He sounded like he meant it. "And then there

was my amazing gift."

"We should go surfing tomorrow. You can try it out."

He made it sound like they were a real couple, with many tomorrows in their future.

"In that case, I should finish my wine and leave you in peace." She forced a laugh. "You must be sick of the Robb clan, all of us, by now."

"I enjoyed myself," he said. "The dynamics are easier to handle when you're not part of the backstory."

"I bet your family doesn't have near the drama mine does."

"Are you kidding? Every family has its share. All my sisters resented me because not only was I a boy, I was the baby. They thought our parents were too soft on me. Kind of the way Theresa feels about Emily."

She straightened to face him. "What about Theresa and Emily?"

"You were probably so busy being the middle child, the peacekeeper, you never noticed it. But I overheard Theresa making a few pointed remarks, implying how easy everything's been for Emily. No one has the same expectations for the baby as they do for the oldest. Did you know Theresa figured the only way to get out from under your parents' thumb was to get married? She would have been disowned if she moved in with Dave, yet years later, when Emily and Michael lived together, no one said a word. She also felt the pressure because your folks wanted grandchildren. Like it was all up to her. You couldn't commit and Emily's too selfish."

"Theresa told you all this?"

"Not in so many words. I got some of it from Dave. He's crazy about Theresa and the kids, but he's pretty frustrated with the way she treats him."

Meredith was silent. Could there be truth in what Asher said?

Asher gave her arm a companionable squeeze. "Hey, when you meet my sisters, they'll will have stories where you think they're talking about someone else entirely."

He said 'when', not 'if'. As if they were really a couple, not just pretending.

"I'm not so sure about surfing tomorrow. It's my family's last day here. I should probably spend it with them."

"They booked an all-day excursion through the hotel. Your mom told me we deserved some time alone."

"My mom said that?"

Asher nodded. "She feels bad for barging in on us unannounced. Said they've monopolized our time enough."

"My *mother* said that?" Meredith narrowed her gaze. "You must have really turned on the charm."

"I was just being myself," Asher said modestly.

She gave him a searching look. Did he really believe that? Was he unaware how women of all ages fell hard for him? Something she'd fought for years, trying her best to stay immune, yet here she was, more than a little in love with the guy, half wishing this play date was real. Every aspect of it! And as he put his arm around her and pulled her head to his shoulder, she consoled herself that for tonight, at least, it was real.

* * *

She woke the next morning all relaxed and sated and reached for Asher but found his side of the bed empty. In the kitchen a note was propped against the coffee pot.

Putting out a fire. Back soon! Love A

She stared at the word love, telling herself not to read anything into it. It was probably just his way of signing off, the way some folks said 'cheers' or 'ciao.'

She poured herself a coffee and wandered onto the lanai with her phone in her other hand. What kind of fire did Asher suddenly need to put out? Was his assistant pulling the same kinds of stunts as Chloe?

Speaking of Chloe, she should see what sort of nonsense her assistant had been posting these last few days. She logged into her account, then froze as she stared at the screen in disbelief. She recovered enough to scroll through, the stories and accusations a blur, but one point was front and center. Resort Wedding Planner has a history of leaving her own groom at the altar. Four times!

She rose so quickly she nearly spilled her coffee. This must be the fire Asher was trying to put out. A little late for that! How dare he break a confidence!

She dashed away the threat of tears as she drove to the hotel. She ought to have known better than to let him close. To share her secrets. She'd done what she'd sworn not to, fallen for that Asher charm, believed the things he said and did. Now her career was ruined and Chloe was having the time of her life with the residue.

The hotel lobby was quiet this early and no one saw her as she headed for the stairs to the executive offices. Halfway up, she ran into Asher coming down. He saw her at the same time she saw him. They both froze. Asher recovered first and loped down to her level.

She gave him a hard look. "What are you doing here?"

He had the good grace to look uncomfortable. "Asking Chloe to rescind her story."

"Haven't you done enough already?"

"I'm not sure what you mean. Joel told me what she was up to and I was hoping to talk some sense into her before the story went viral."

Meredith crossed her arms over her chest. "I take back everything I said earlier. We'll never be friends. Friends don't tell tales, especially when the story is destined to destroy the other person."

"Mer, I—"

"Originally, I asked you to break up with me in front of my family, but I'm saving you the trouble. We are over! Friendship finished. Fake relationship done. Fuck friends over. All of it!"

She pulled away from him and ran down the steps to the lobby, leaving Asher on the landing.

"Meredith?"

Halfway across the lobby she stumbled in shock at the familiar voice, the familiar face."

"Zack! What are you doing here?"

Her former fiancée gave a sheepish grin.

"Looking for you."

"Zack—"

"Not like that," he said quickly. "I'm here on my honeymoon. But some chick named Chloe has been messaging me asking me about our break up. Her social media page said she works here as well, and I didn't know how else to get hold of you and warn you."

Meredith searched the face of the man she'd once planned to spend her life with. "What did you tell her?"

"Nothing. I wanted to talk to you first."

Meredith felt the color slowly coming back into her face as her breathing slowed and her heart rate returned to something near normal.

Zack gave her a concerned look. "You'd better sit down before you fall over. I didn't mean to surprise you like this. I was going to leave a note with the concierge."

"Honeymoon," she said, once she could speak. "That's great. I'm really happy for you. I—I never meant to hurt you the way I did."

"We both know I took things harder than I should have," Zack said.

Meredith swallowed thickly, aware Zack was referring to the handful of pills he took after she called off their wedding. She'd been the one to find him and call 911.

"I met my wife at a support group for jilted partners. So, in a way you brought the two of us together. She's really great. I'd like you to meet her one day."

Meredith smiled. "I don't think your honeymoon would be the appropriate time."

"Of course not." Zack glanced at his watch. "Speaking of honeymoons, I'd better get back. I just wanted to warn you about that Chloe woman. And to say thank you." He gave her a quick hug. "If it wasn't for you, I never would have met my soul mate."

Meredith nodded, aware that around her, the lobby was coming to life. She needed to get out of there before her family showed up and saw her. She was just about to open her car door when she caught sight of her reflection in the door's window. She stopped to take a good, long look. Is this the way she wanted her life here to play out? Did she want to spend her life following her old, familiar pattern of running away? Boyfriends. Family. Jobs. Anything unpleasant.

Instead of opening the vehicle's door, she turned and went back inside the hotel. Her first stop was Mr. Yoshi's office. The GM lived on site and even though it was the day after Christmas, his job was his life and she knew he'd be hard at it. His receptionist's desk was empty so she went to his office door and knocked.

"Come."

She wiped her sweaty palms on her shorts and stepped inside.

Chapter 10

"Meredith." Mr. Yoshi frowned as he took in her casual attire. "Are you back from vacation?"

"No," she said. "But something came up that I need to talk to you about. It won't take long."

He closed his laptop and indicated the chair across the desk from him. Meredith perched on the edge.

Mr. Yoshi folded his hands on the desk in front of him. "Are your family members not enjoying themselves?"

"It's nothing like that," she said. "Their stay here has been perfect. Thank you for allowing me to spend time with them."

He nodded. "We're a 'family first' corporation."

"I love being an event planner here," she said in a rush. "I love all of it, especially the weddings."

He frowned. "You're not leaving us, are you?"

"That all depends." She watched his eyes

flicker as he digested her words. "I don't want to leave, but it might be necessary."

He raised his chin and waited.

"Back in Seattle, I was engaged. More than once in fact."

If he was feeling impatient, you wouldn't know it. He'd always been a good listener. Part of what made him a great boss.

"I'm afraid it might not look good for the hotel if guests were to learn you have a wedding planner who never managed to follow through with her own weddings."

"What does one thing have to do with the other?"

"Nothing really. My background in no way impedes my ability to do my job. But social media can really blow these things out of proportion and I'm afraid—"

"Are you aware that customer reviews on all the travel sites nearly always mention you by name? You're the best events planner this resort has ever had. I don't know what you're worried about, but—"

"Someone on the staff has been posting messages to try and discredit me."

He sat up straight, his eyes boring into hers. "Do you know who this person is?"

She nodded.

"Then I suggest you work it out with them. There will be no infighting among my staff members. And no undermining each other, is that clear?"

She nodded and stood. "Yes, Mr. Yoshi."

He stood as well. "I knew when I hired you that Chloe would resent being passed over for the position. But she was too young and didn't have the experience or maturity for the job. I've admired the way you've mentored her in spite of her resentment. But if word of unprofessional behavior on her part happened to get around the island to the other resorts, she will have effectively destroyed her chances for an event planning job in the future. You might share that with her."

"That's an excellent point," Meredith said. "I'd

hate to see my protégé accidentally shoot herself in the foot."

Mr. Yoshi rounded the desk and extended his hand. "Merry Christmas, Meredith. Give my best to your family. Your mother and I had quite the conversation."

Meredith nodded. "Thank you. I will."

* * *

Back at home, Meredith was proud of herself for breaking old patterns. She still had to deal with Chloe, but it could wait. Luckily, she'd left the new surfboard at Asher's. Hopefully he could return it. As long as they both worked at the resort they were bound to cross paths from time to time, but she'd do her best to see it wasn't often. Maybe, as time passed, it wouldn't even hurt.

Seeing Zack today and hearing he was happy was another reason to let go of her past. Let go of her guilt. As far as her family went, she knew exactly what she planned to say when she saw them off tomorrow.

She changed her strategy a dozen times during

the day and the night before she showed up at the hotel the next morning. The clan was gathered in the lobby. Theresa wore an elastic support on her ankle. The kids looked sunburned and happy.

"There you are," her mother said, as she looked past Meredith. "Isn't Asher coming to see us off as well?"

"Actually, he's not," she said. "Let's step outside for a sec before you leave."

Outside, the temperature was already climbing. Her mother faced her with a bit of a hangdog look. "I'm sorry if I came across as too pushy, barging in unannounced at your place of work, but I'm really glad we came. It was so refreshing to see you and Asher, how easy you are with each other."

"About that," Meredith said, staring at the ground. They all watched her expectantly. Theresa smirked, as if she already knew what Meredith was about to say. "We're easy with each other because we've been friends for almost three years."

"And don't they say friendship is the best basis for a solid relationship?" Helen said.

She shook her head. "There is no relationship between Asher and I. I made it all up. Asher went along with it because he's just that kind of guy."

"But—" Her mother looked puzzled. "You were at his place that morning we showed up looking for you."

"Yeah, well… It was all part of the ruse."

"Quite the act," Theresa drawled. "Although personally, I had a hard time believing you could snag a guy like that."

"A guy like what?" Dave chimed up. "A decent guy? A guy who clearly cares for her?" He turned to Meredith. "Maybe your friendship is meant to be more."

"Unfortunately, the friendship is over," Meredith said. "I found out yesterday that he betrayed a confidence. Asher told my assistant about my past engagements and she used that information to discredit me on social media, hoping to get me fired so she could have my job."

For once her family members were silent as they exchanged looks among themselves.

Theresa grew unnaturally pale. Finally, she spoke. "You might want to rethink blaming Asher for that."

"He's the only one I told," Meredith said. "When he learned what she was up to, he beat a hasty path here to talk to her. To get her to take down her posts before I saw them."

"Um, Mer." Theresa looked shamefaced. "I might have accidentally said something to your assistant."

"*You did?*"

"That day I was talking to her. I'm sorry, I didn't mean to let it slip, but somehow I did. I guess I've always been a little jealous of you. Glam job, glam life. Good at everything you do. Then you move here and land a great guy with no repercussions for the string of broken hearts you left behind."

Helen turned to Theresa. "You have no reason to be jealous of your sister. Most women would kill for what you have. A stable life with a great husband and children."

Theresa was suddenly busy studying her feet. "That doesn't mean someone else's grass doesn't look greener."

Dave put his arm around his wife. "I love you, babe. And if there's something missing from your life with us, we'll all work together to make sure you have whatever makes you happy. Isn't that right kids?" At Dave's urging the youngsters joined their parents, hanging on their arms.

Emily sidled forward. "You know how you were bugging me about not having kids? Saying I was too selfish? The truth is, we've been trying. But nothing happened. I'm booked to see a specialist next month to find out what the problem is. There's a chance I may never be a mother."

Theresa's eyes widened. She looked at their mom. "Did you know?"

"I found out a short time ago," Helen admitted.

"You should have said something. I never would have—" She grabbed Emily in a huge hug. "I've been a selfish bitch. Please forgive me."

As Meredith watched her sisters crying and

hugging, her dad moved to her side. "It looks like our family really needed this vacation."

Meredith nodded and gave him a quick hug. "All of us."

"You're sure you and Asher—?"

She shook her head. "I'll apologize for jumping to conclusions. Maybe given time, we can renew some sort of friendship." Even as she said it out loud, she knew it wasn't going to happen. Even if he forgave her she couldn't hang out with Asher, pretend to be his friend, watch him date other women. It would hurt too much.

"Tell him I said it was nice to meet him. We all really enjoyed his company."

"I'll pass that along."

Eventually the family was loaded into the airport shuttle and on their way. Meredith turned and headed for the stairs to her office. Time to have a serious conversation with Chloe.

* * *

Asher stared at the surfboard propped under the Christmas tree, its presence a mocking reminder of what he'd almost had with Meredith. She'd been an intriguing puzzle, but not one he was meant to fully figure out. He'd gone back to work earlier that day, relieved to see Chloe had removed all the media posts. She must have listened when he'd told her it was the right thing to do.

Christmas might be over, but the resort was busier than ever, gearing up for New Year's Eve and all the accompanying festivities. He hadn't seen hide nor hair of Meredith, which was just as well. He'd turned her down flat when she asked to see him, and eventually had received a text where she apologized for jumping to the wrong conclusion, adding her sister had been the one to spill the goods to Chloe.

With a push of the send button, he'd accepted her apology. The same as he accepted that things between them were over. He'd been a great fake boyfriend, but he was kidding himself if he'd ever thought the role was about to become permanent. Meredith's track record spoke for itself. And no one could say he hadn't been warned.

Spending Christmas day with the Robb family had made him miss his own family in a serious way. There was something comforting about going home to unconditional love and support, a place where you didn't need to be someone you weren't.

* * *

Meredith opened her fridge door, then closed it again. She wasn't hungry. Her appetite had disappeared long before she received Ash's two-word text. *Apology accepted.*

Her condo felt confining, especially when she recalled the welcoming homey feel at Asher's. Meredith hated to admit to herself just how much she missed him. No matter where she was, she had one eye out for him, hungry for even a glimpse: around the resort or driving past their favorite surf beach.

Come to think of it, she hadn't seen his Jeep in the staff parking lot the past two days. She hoped he wasn't sick. It was out of her way, but she drove by his house on her way to work on the morning of New Year's Eve. No sign of his vehicle there, either.

When she reached work, her heart gave a happy hiccup at the sight of his Jeep pulling in ahead of her. With a casualness she was far from feeling, she parked a few cars over, hoping for a brief glimpse as he got out of his Jeep. But when the driver's door opened, out stepped Joel, Asher's assistant. She hurriedly grabbed her briefcase and followed him to the storage sheds that housed the recreation equipment. What if Asher was sick? In the hospital, even.

"Joel," she called, breathless by the time she caught up to him outside the sheds.

He turned, gave her a cool look and kept going.

"Joel. Wait up."

He didn't look pleased as he turned toward her.

"I saw you drive up in Ash's Jeep. Is he okay?'

Joel's gaze hardened. How much did he know? She recalled that he'd seen her and Asher together as a fake couple when her family was here.

"I haven't seen him for a few days," she added, afraid he wasn't going to answer her.

"He's fine," Joel said curtly, and started to turn away.

"Wait," she pleaded. "I don't know what he told you about pretending to be my boyfriend, but—"

"He's the real deal you know," Joel said in a rush. "The last of the good guys who'd do anything for anybody, even if it turned out they were only using him and weren't gracious enough to appreciate everything he did."

"I know that," Meredith said. "That's why I need to talk to him."

"You're too late," Joel said. "I just dropped him at the airport. He's on his way to spend New Year's with his family. He didn't say so exactly, but I'm pretty sure he didn't want to be around here and run into you."

"He's on his way to Florida!" Meredith's heart landed down near her knees with a heavy flop. "Not for good, surely."

"He didn't say when he'd be back. He asked me to keep his Jeep and check on his place."

Meredith barely heard what Joel said over the rushing sound in her ears. *Asher was leaving. Asher was leaving.*

He couldn't leave! Not with the way things were between them!

"Which airline?" she asked.

"Why?" Joel said.

"Just tell me which airline he's flying."

* * *

Meredith broke every speed limit on the way to the airport. The departure parking lot was nearly empty and she snagged the closest spot she saw, then raced to the terminal, praying she was in time. That he hadn't been through security yet. This time of year, most of the travelers were coming to the island, not leaving.

It was quiet inside, with only one ticket agent open, looking after a handful of passengers, one of whom was Asher. She watched the agent hand Asher his boarding pass, saw him pick up his backpack and head for the security screening.

She raced the length of the building, dodging

anyone in her way. "Ash!" she called. Her voice echoed through the nearly empty terminal. He turned. His face changed when he saw her; a guarded look took the place of his usual carefree, easy grin. She skidded to a stop a few feet away. Had she done that? Hurt Ash the way she'd hurt all the other men who had once cared about her?

"I'm sorry," she said.

"I already accepted your apology."

"Joel said you're going home to see your family. Will you be away long?"

"Depends."

He stepped out of the way of a group of people headed for the security screening.

"I was worried about you," she said, taking several tentative steps closer. "I missed you," she added when he made no comment. She watched a muscle jump in his jaw and wondered if he had clenched his teeth.

"This is a switch. Don't you usually run away from the guy you just dumped? Or is this time different because I was only a fake boyfriend?"

"This time is different," she said, low-voiced. "This time I didn't want it to be over. I wanted it to be real. To be forever."

"What are you trying to say?"

"I think it started back when we first met. I tried to deny feeling anything special. A feeling I never had before. It scared me and I kidded myself into thinking we could be friends." She licked her lips and took a deep breath. "It was shockingly easy to tell my family that you were my guy. It didn't even feel like a lie. And then, suddenly, fake wasn't enough. I wanted it all. I wanted 'us' to be real, to make plans for the future. Our future. I had no urge to run." His expression didn't change or soften as she rambled on. "And I didn't want you to leave before I had the chance to tell you that."

His gaze narrowed. "What's different?"

"I am. I'm different with you. I'm better with you. I'm who I'm supposed to be when I'm with you. And you accepted me as I was, screwed up and confused and neurotic. You just accepted me."

"Is that so surprising?"

"It's the first time in my life I didn't feel I had to compromise, to pretend to be whoever the other person expected me to. Nothing to this point has felt so right or been such a perfect fit."

He continued to eye her. "Are you saying you've changed?"

"I have. Really. And when you get back, if you'd just give me the chance to prove it—"

"How about now?"

She tensed, aware his eyes held a challenge. "What about now?"

"Come with me."

"What? Now? Oh I—"

He smiled ruefully. "Haven't made a dozen lists of what to pack and what needs to be taken care of? Just come. Right now. Prove what you just said is true. That you're different with me. That you're better with me. Let's see this new you."

She hitched her shoulder bag higher. "Do I have time to buy a toothbrush?"

He smiled. His eyes took on that warm,

intimate look that curled her toes. When he opened his arms she threw herself at him, hanging on as if she'd never let go.

He kissed her and her insides turned to mushy jelly. This was real. Ash was real. *They* were real!

It was much later when the kiss ended and she looked up at him, wondering if he could see the love shining from her eyes as she cradled his face between her hands.

He felt so good. So familiar. *So hers!*

"What will your family say when I arrive unannounced?"

"I'm pretty sure they'll love you as much as I do. After they finish giving you the third degree, and before they start recounting mortifying stories about me when I was young."

She snugged her arm around his waist as they headed back to the ticket counter. "I love you, Ash." She giggled. "I can't wait to tell my family. They won't believe it."

He smiled down at her. "What's not to believe? They thought we were perfect together right from the start."

She loved the way they fit together. Even their stride matched. "Yeah, but who knew they were right?"

"I did," Ash said smugly. "I'm just glad you came around."

"Do you always need to get in the last word?"

"Always."

DEAR READER...

Thank you for picking up a copy of *No Groom at The Inn.* If you enjoyed reading it, please tell others by leaving a review wherever you purchased it or on Goodreads or BookBub.

If you're looking for more sweet, contemporary feel-good Christmas Romances, check out *Holly's Wish*, a story about wishing, and the Magic of Christmas in the small town of Dickens.

Fake dating is alive and well in *One Fantasy Fall* where a Hollywood Stuntman clashes with a well-meaning, small town, small island girl, a Blue Sky Island Romance.   Here's a taste:

Excerpt: One Fantasy Fall

Kaitlin wasn't sure if the rushing sound in her ears was due to the waterfall behind her or a defense mechanism for the way Blaze was looking at her. She shivered as they exchanged looks, not one stranger to another, but something far more intimate. So powerful she could almost believe he meant what he said.

"Will you be at the tournament tomorrow?"

She nodded. "I got a press pass so I can pretend to be busy and important."

Blaze took her arm. "Speaking of busy and important, we should get back to the party." He brushed her lips with his thumb smearing her lipstick and giving her hair a tousle.

"What are you doing?"

"Giving people a reason to speculate where we snuck off to together. And why."

She swallowed thickly, response impossible given the way her heart was fluttering in her throat. Blaze was a little too good at this fake date stuff. For a second there, it felt like he cared.

* * *

You might have guessed I write mainly about cowboys, Wild West and Contemporary Times, with the occasional playboy thrown in for good measure.

See more on my website: KathleenLawless.com

MORE FROM KATHLEEN

Sweet Western Historical Romance
THE SPINSTER TAKES A GROOM SERIES
The Gambler
The Magician

Western Historical Romance
Grace's Folly
Anora's Pride
Callie's Honor
Maddy's Fugitive
Widows, Babies and Brides (Box Set of all 4)

Sweet Western Historical Romance
SEVEN BRIDES FOR SEVEN BROTHERS
SERIES
Brody's Bride - Book 1
Bradley's Bride - Book 2
Braydon's Bride - Book 3
Blake's Bride - Book 4
Bishop's Bride - Book 5
Barron's Bride - Book 6
Benjamin's Bride - Book 7
Seven Brides for Seven Brothers Box Set 1 -
Prequel & Books 1 to 3
Seven Brides for Seven Brothers Box Set 2 - Books
4 to 7
Sweet Western Historical Romance

WIDOWS OF THE WILD WEST
Hope
Janie

Sweet Western Historical Romance
MAIL ORDER BRIDES
Mail Order Olivia
Mail Order Rachel
Mail Order Martina
A Bride for Shane
A Bride for Riley
A Bride for Weston
Mail Order Noelle
Chelsea's Choice
Lila: Rescue Me Mail Order Brides
Here Come the Brides Volume 1
Here Come the Brides Volume 2

Sweet Contemporary Romance
Frannie (Always a Bridesmaid)
Baxter (Last Man Standing)
Blue Sky Island
One Cinderella Spring
One Stolen Summer
One Fantasy Fall
One Wondrous Winter

Sweet Christmas Romance Novellas
Holly's Wish

No Groom at the Inn

Women's Fiction
Fabulous at Fifty

Romantic Suspense
Final Heat

Afterburn

Steamy Historical Romance
Taboo

Unmasked

Reckless Rogues - Box Set of the 2 Books

Steamy Contemporary Romance
SECRET SEDUCTIONS
Her Untamed Cowboy - Book 1

Her Undercover Cowboy - Book 2

Her Unwilling Cowboy - Book 3

Who Needs a Cowboy! - Book 4

Intimate Strangers

* * *

To hear about Kathleen's new releases, special fan pricing sales, and also receive a free book, sign up for her VIP Reader Newsletter. You can find the sign-up link on her website at KathleenLawless.com

ABOUT THE AUTHOR

USA Today Bestselling Author Kathleen Lawless blames a misspent youth watching Rawhide, Maverick and Bonanza for her fascination with cowboys, which doesn't stop her from creating a wide variety of interests and occupations for her many alpha male heroes.

With over 50 published novels to her credit, she enjoys pushing the boundaries of traditional romance into historical romance, contemporary romance, romantic suspense and women's fiction.

She makes her home in the Pacific Northwest and loves to hear from her readers.

* * *

Where to find Kathleen:
KathleenLawless.com
Goodreads | BookBub
Facebook | Instagram | TikTok